Read All About BUGS

by Mae Respicio

PEBBLE
a capstone imprint

Published by Pebble, an imprint of Capstone
1710 Roe Crest Drive, North Mankato, Minnesota 56003
capstonepub.com

Library of Congress Cataloging-in-Publication Data
Names: Respicio, Mae, author.
Title: Read all about bugs / by Mae Respicio.
Description: North Mankato, Minnesota : Pebble, an imprint of Capstone, [2023] | Series: Read all about it | Includes index. | Audience: Ages 5-8 | Audience: Grades K-1 | Summary: "Bugs are everywhere! From large beetles to tiny gnats, bugs come in a variety of sizes, colors, and shapes. Find out all about bug types, behaviors, life cycles, and more in this fact-filled book. Stunning photos give readers an up-close look at bugs-big and small!"— Provided by publisher.
Identifiers: LCCN 2022024852 (print) | LCCN 2022024853 (ebook) | ISBN 9780756572549 (hardcover) | ISBN 9780756573379 (paperback) | ISBN 9780756572518 (eBook PDF) | ISBN 9780756572532 (kindle edition)
Subjects: LCSH: Insects—Juvenile literature.
Classification: LCC QL467.2 .R47 2023 (print) | LCC QL467.2 (ebook) | DDC 595.7—dc23/eng/20220608
LC record available at https://lccn.loc.gov/2022024852
LC ebook record available at https://lccn.loc.gov/2022024853

Image Credits
Shutterstock: A. Kehinde, bottom, 18, aabeele, middle, 9, AG-PHOTOS, bottom, 9, Akos Nagy, bottom 7, AlibabaArt, top, 18, Andrii Oleksiienko, top, 6, benvl photography, 16, Berna Namoglu, bottom, 29, Candy_Plus, middle, 21, Cathy Keifer, top, 19, ChameleonsEye, 24, Darkdiamond67, top, 13, David James Chatterton, bottom, 15, Digital Images Studio, top right cover, efendy, top, 9, frank60, top, 22, Gianfranco Vivi, bottom, 22, Ihor Hvozdetskyi, bottom, 23, Jay Ondreicka, middle, 5, JO2, 20, khlungcenter, top, 23, Kritchai7752, middle, 29, Landshark1, top, 15, Lynda Hayes, top, 25, MarcelClemens, bottom, 6, Mark Brandon, bottom cover, 1, top, 7, bottom, 25, Minko Peev, top, 29, Mr. Background, middle, 11, Omksmile, 26, Ondrej Prosicky, top, 27, ploypemuk, bottom, 19, top, 21, PomInPerth, top, 10, Porco_Rosso, bottom, 17, Protasov AN, top, 5, reisegraf.ch, middle, 25, Risto Puranen, bottom, 21, Salparadis, 8, Silvia Dubois, top, 17, skydie, top, 11, skynetphoto, middle, 13, smspsy, middle, 4, Srinivasan.Clicks, middle, 23, Stefan Rotter, middle, 30, Stephan Morris, bottom, 10, Studiotouch, 28, sumikophoto, middle, 17, tcareob72, bottom, 14, Tomasz Klejdysz, 12, vainillaychile, bottom, 13, Wolfgang Schmid, bottom, 30, yamaoyaji, top, 30, Yan Lv, bottom, 11, YapAhock, bottom, 4, yod 67, bottom, 5, bottom, 27, Young Swee Ming, top, 14

Editorial Credits
Editor: Carrie Sheely; Designer: Bobbie Nuytten; Media Researcher: Donna Metcalf; Production Specialist: Tori Abraham

Printed in the United States 5553

Table of Contents

Words in **bold** are in the glossary.

Chapter 1

What Are Bugs?

Bugs! They creep, crawl, buzz, and bite. Many people use the word "bug" to mean any kind of small crawling or flying creature. But only some bugs are **insects**. Let's learn more about bugs!

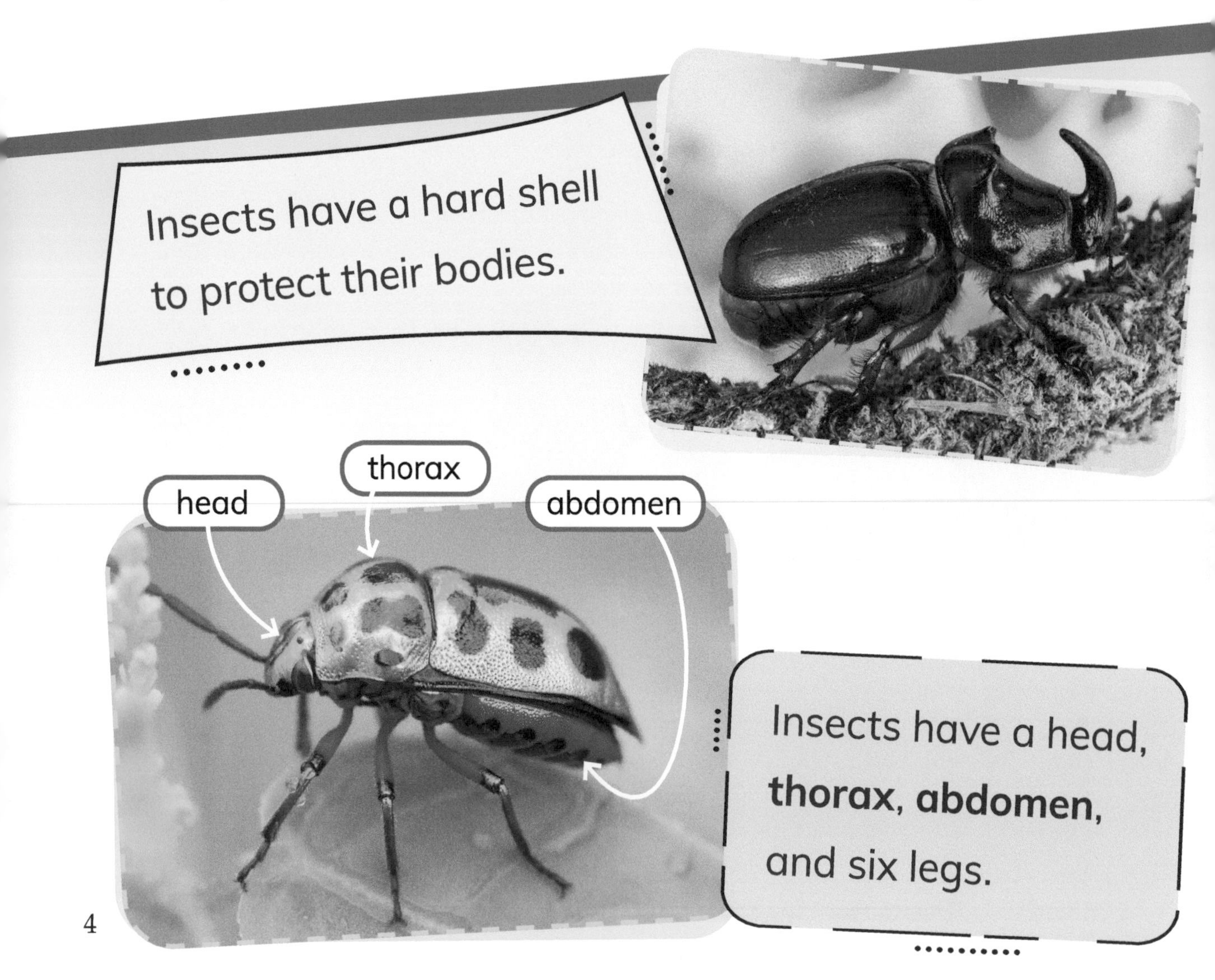

Insects are the largest group of animals on Earth.

Some insects are true bugs. They have straw-shaped mouth parts to suck juices.

Bugs live in every part of the world.

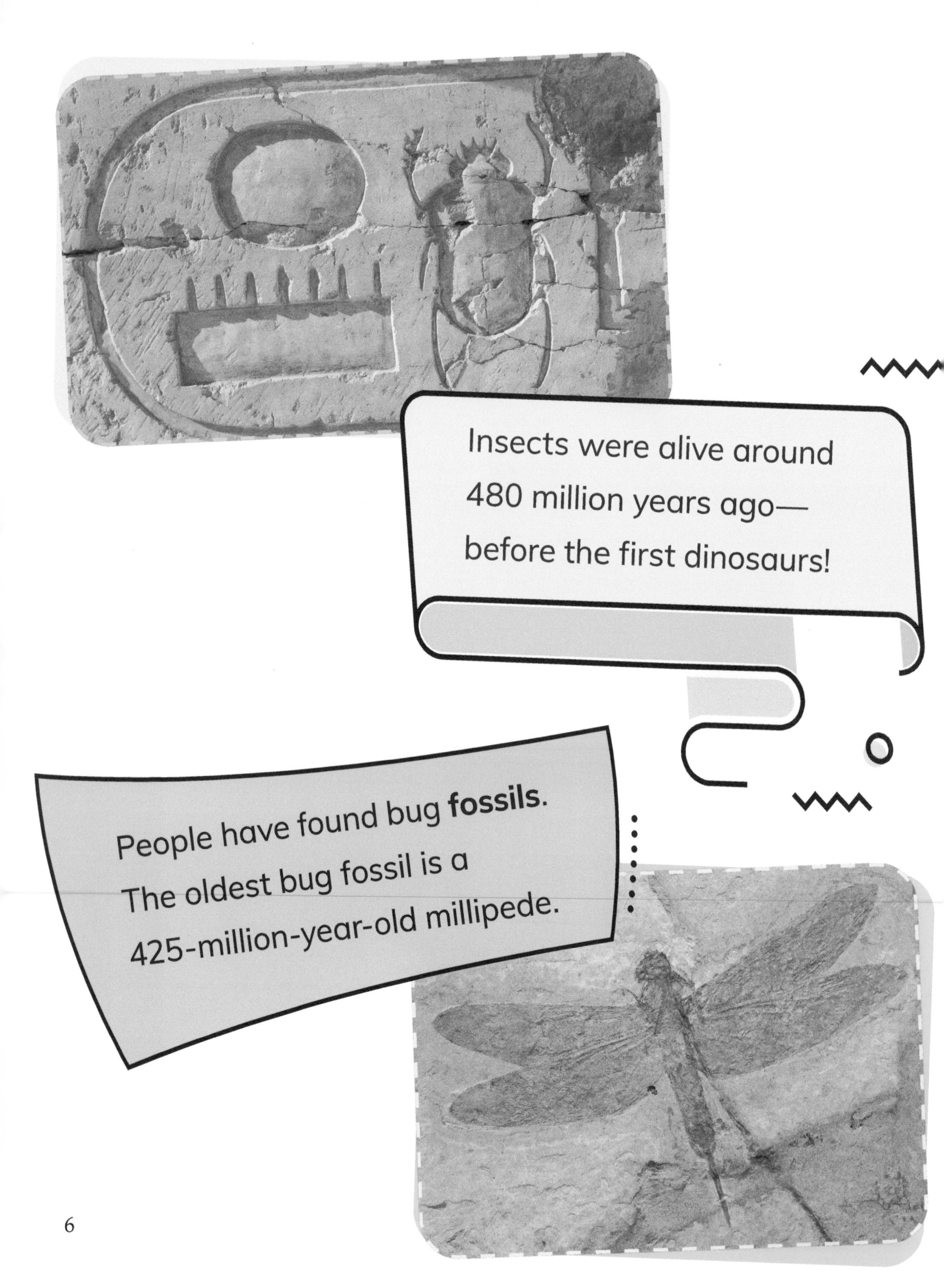

Insects were alive around 480 million years ago—before the first dinosaurs!

People have found bug **fossils**. The oldest bug fossil is a 425-million-year-old millipede.

People first began using “bugs” to describe insects in the 1600s.

The bedbug was likely the first insect to be called a “bug.”

Chapter 2

Kinds of Bugs

There are around 10 quintillion insects (10,000,000,000,000,000,000) on Earth. So far, scientists have found about 900,000 different kinds. But there could be many more that are still unknown!

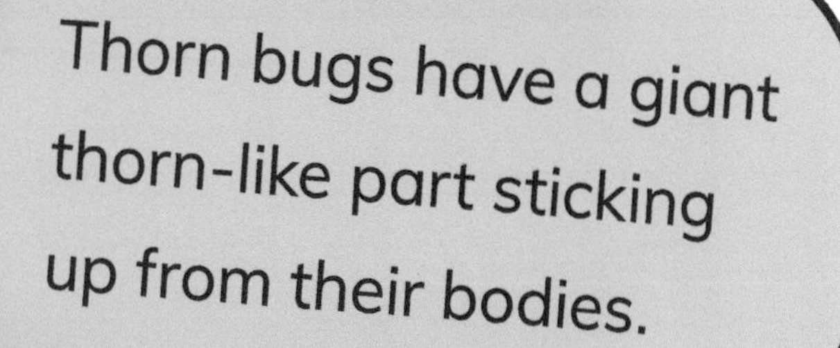

Dung beetles can roll balls of poop that are over 50 times their own body weight.

Hummingbird hawk-moths hover in the air like hummingbirds.

Ants and other social insects live in groups called colonies.

The red spotted jewel beetle has six spots on its shimmery wings.

Water striders can walk on water.

The giant burrowing cockroach is the biggest cockroach. It can weigh about as much as a golf ball.

Honeybees buzz, but they can also quack and toot.

Goliath beetles can be as big as your palm.

Chapter 3

Bug Life Stages

Young bugs grow by going through changes. Some insects have four life stages: egg, **larva**, **pupa**, and adult. Others have three: egg, nymph, and adult.

An army ant queen can lay 300,000 eggs in a few days.

Nymphs look a lot like the adults they will become.

Caterpillars are butterfly or moth larvae.

Cicadas shed their hard outside covering, or **molt**, as they grow.

Jumping bean moth caterpillars grow inside seed pods of a shrub. The pods appear to jump!

A queen termite can live up to 50 years.

Butterfly caterpillars change inside a **chrysalis** during the pupa stage.

Moth caterpillars grow inside a **cocoon** during the pupa stage.

Some insect nymphs live in water, but the adults fly on land.

Chapter 4

Bug Bodies

Bugs come in all shapes, colors, and sizes. Their body parts can be different. Some have wings, while others have no wings. Some have two eyes. Others have up to five!

A cricket has tiny ears on the front of its legs.

Grasshoppers jump with their hind legs and walk with their front ones.

Honeybees beat their wings about 200 times per second.

The sound of a bee buzzing comes from how fast it beats its wings.

A cockroach can live for many days without its head.
The Picasso bug was named after the painter Pablo Picasso.

Many moths have **antennae** that look like feathers.

Most caterpillars have 12 eyes, but they have bad eyesight.

Chapter 5

Bug Senses

Bugs have five senses like people do. They hear, taste, see, touch, and smell by using their body parts.

Moths smell each other to find a mate.

Dragonflies have big compound eyes that can see in nearly all directions.

A butterfly can see more colors than people.

Dragonflies can fly backward.

One way mosquitoes find humans to bite is by smelling their breath.

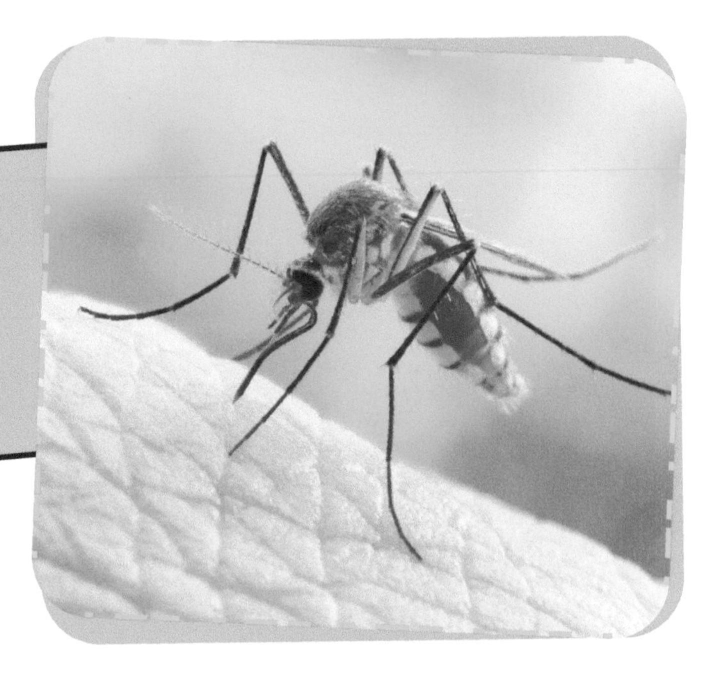

Blue morpho butterflies have ears on their wings.

Lightning bugs glow in the dark to communicate with one another.

Houseflies taste with their feet.

The greater wax moth can hear the highest-**pitched** sounds of any animal.

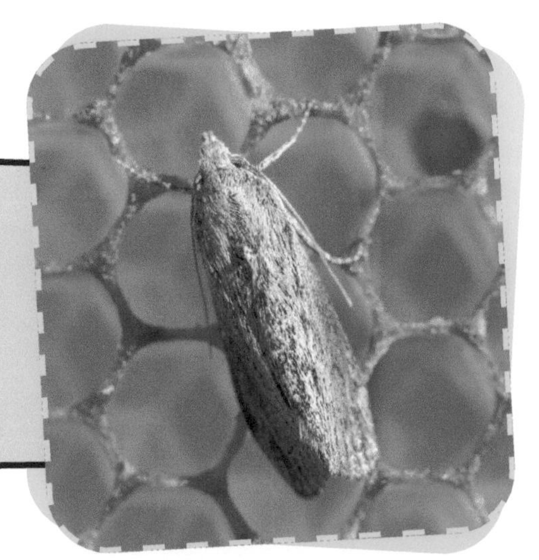

Chapter 6

Bug Survival

Bugs need food, water, and the right living conditions to survive. They also have to stay safe from **predators** that try to eat them.

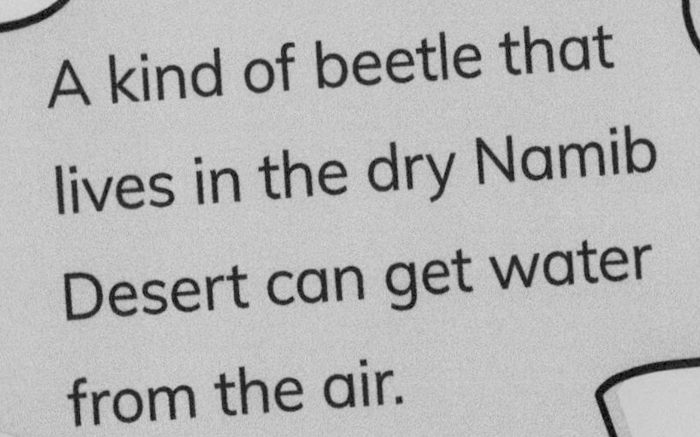

Some caterpillars can make themselves look like snakes to scare away attackers.

Some insects travel to warm places during winter to escape the cold.

Walking sticks stay hidden by looking like sticks on trees.

To trick birds, ladybugs can play dead.

Most bees get food from plants. But some stingless bees eat meat.

A monarch butterfly's colors warn predators that it is poisonous.

If a female cuckoo wasp is threatened, it can roll into a ball and stay protected by its armor plates.

Chapter 7

Bugs and Us

Insects have helped humans in many different ways throughout history. We all need bugs!

Fruit flies were the first living creatures sent into space.

Some insects help break down the bodies of dead animals. They keep forests clean.

Honeybees help new plants grow by leaving pollen behind. This helps us have blueberries, apples, and other foods to eat.

Biting ants with big jaws were once used to stitch wounds.

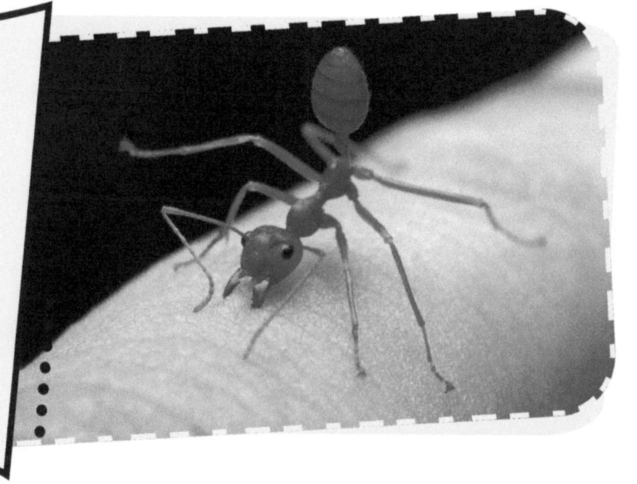

People make silk clothes from the cocoons of silkworm moths.

Maggots can help clean people's wounds.

Ground beetles eat slugs that can ruin gardens.

Some people believe that if a ladybug lands on you, its number of spots is how many years you'll have good luck!

Glossary

abdomen—the back section of an insect's body

antennae—feelers on an insect's head

chrysalis—the hard shell inside which a pupa changes into a butterfly

cocoon—a covering made of silky threads; a moth makes a cocoon to protect itself while it changes from larva to pupa

fossil—the remains or traces of plants and animals that are preserved as rock

insect—a small animal with a hard outer shell, six legs, three body sections, and two antennae; most insects have wings

larva—an insect at the stage of development between an egg and a pupa when it looks like a worm

molt—to shed an outer layer of skin

pitch—how high or low a sound is

predator—an animal that eats another animal for food

pupa—an insect at the stage of development between a larva and an adult

thorax—the middle section of an insect's body; wings and legs are attached to the thorax

Index

About the Author

Mae Respicio is a nonfiction writer and middle grade author whose books include *The House that Lou Built*, which won an Asian Pacific American Libraries Association honor award and was an NPR Best Book. Mae lives with her family in northern California where nearly every morning she gets to see all kinds of beautiful bugs while out hiking with her dog, Riggs. Visit her at maerespicio.com.